For Barb Schneider and her 5th graders. And to my P.A. friends. –Denise

To my many friends at the Columbus Zoo and the people who take care of them. –Tim

Sleeping Bear Press
315 E. Eisenhower Parkway, Suite 200
Ann Arbor, MI 48108
www.sleepingbearpress.com

Printed and bound in the United States.

10 9 8 7 6 5 4 3 2 1

Library of Congress Cataloging-in-Publication Data

Brennan-Nelson, Denise.
   Maestro Stu saves the zoo / written by Denise Brennan-Nelson ; illustrated by Tim Bowers.
   p. cm.
   Summary: Stu has always loved living near a zoo and pretending to conduct the "music" of the animals there, so when he learns that Mr. Cooper is trying to shut the place down, Stu hatches a plan to save his animal friends' home.
   ISBN 978-1-58536-802-0 (hardback)
   [1. Zoos–Fiction. 2. Zoo animals–Fiction. 3. Animal sounds–Fiction. 4. Conductors (Music)–Fiction. 5. English language–Idioms–Fiction.] I. Title.
   PZ7.B75165Mae 2012
   [E]–dc23   2012007575

Maestro Stu SAVES the ZOO

Written by Denise Brennan-Nelson

Illustrated by Tim Bowers

Since he was knee-high to a grasshopper, Stu had been visiting the nearby zoo. He visited so often everyone at the zoo knew him by name, even the animals.

At night, when the zoo was closed, the animals made music. Living only a block away, Stu and Momma could hear them.

Momma called their sounds a symphony. Some nights the tone was soft and low, other times, upbeat and jazzy. She said it was music to her ears and swayed to the beat while Stu played Maestro.

When Stu was tucked into bed snug as a bug in a rug, he would fall asleep to the animals' sounds and dream of the place he loved best.

But time passed and Stu discovered that not everyone loved the animals as much as he and Momma did.

Mr. Cooper wanted to tear the zoo down so he could build a mall.
And he had no use for the animals; they would have to go.

But first he would have to convince the city to sell him the zoo.

Mr. Cooper went to every city meeting. He rubbed elbows with the fat
cats in their ivory tower every chance he got. He padded their pockets,
bought them extravagant gifts, and sent them on expensive trips.

Before long city officials were willing to sell him the zoo.

A press conference was called to announce the sale of the zoo, and reporters came from everywhere to get the news firsthand.

"A mall," Mr. Cooper explained, "will make the city better."

When a reporter asked him about the animals, he brushed them off. "They're not my concern. They're just animals."

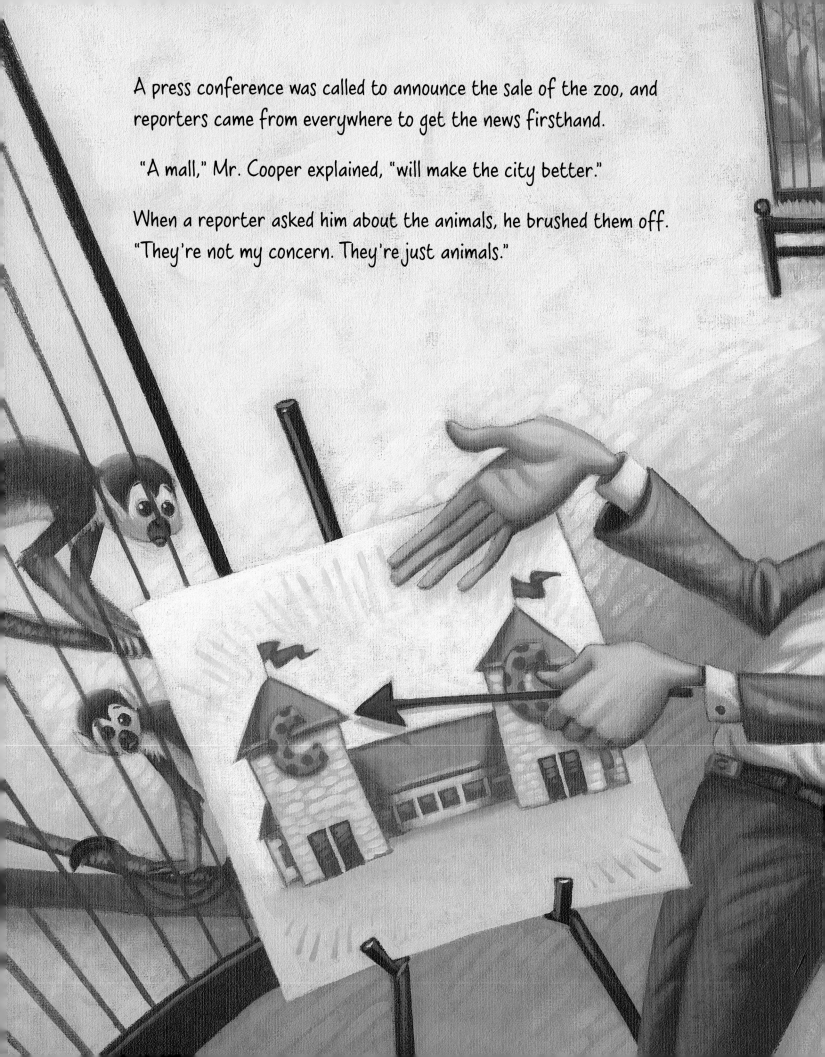

From their cages the animals watched and listened in disbelief.

Doom and gloom settled over the zoo like a thick blanket of fog as the animals realized they were going to lose their home.

Lion took the bull by the horns. He sent out a memo to every creature in the zoo announcing an emergency meeting.

Late that night, while the security guard was taking a catnap, the animals gathered to discuss the news.

They were in an uproar!

Polar Bear was coming apart at the seams.

"Pull yourself together," Rhino said.

Lion took control. "Calm down, everyone!"

The sloths yawned, "Aren't we making a mountain out of a molehill?"

"Get your head out of the clouds!" Tiger said. "They're selling our home! That man is going to get rid of us!"

Emu cried, "We're goners."

Giraffe went weak at the knees.

Ram tried to get a grip on himself.

And Gazelle, who always wore her heart on her sleeve, sobbed, "We have to do something!"

Stu couldn't keep quiet any longer and stepped out of the shadows.

"Well, I'll be a monkey's uncle," Ape said, when he laid eyes on the boy.

"Stu, what are you doing here at this hour?" Elephant asked.

Stu held up the memo. "I found this. I came to help."

"Can you save our home?" they asked him.

"No, but you can," he said.

"What can we do?" Wildebeest said. "We're just animals."

"Yeah, our hands are tied," said the penguins, shaking their heads.

"I have an idea," Stu said. "I know what you can do."

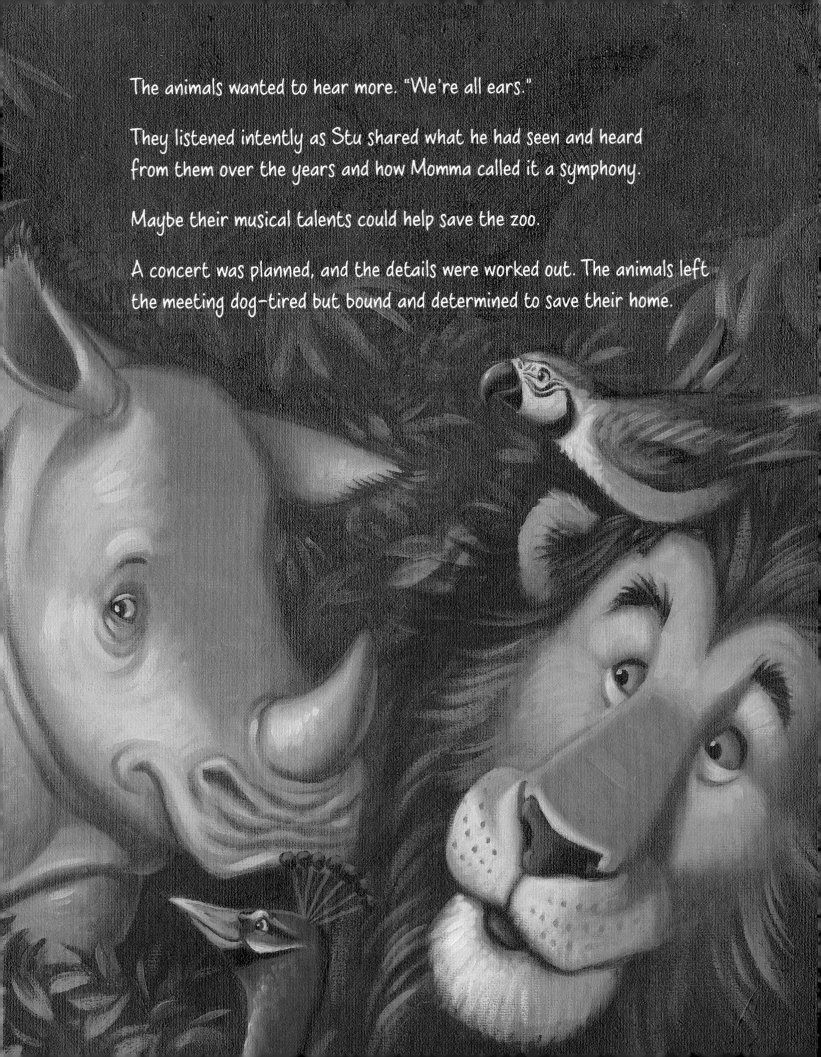

The animals wanted to hear more. "We're all ears."

They listened intently as Stu shared what he had seen and heard from them over the years and how Momma called it a symphony.

Maybe their musical talents could help save the zoo.

A concert was planned, and the details were worked out. The animals left the meeting dog-tired but bound and determined to save their home.

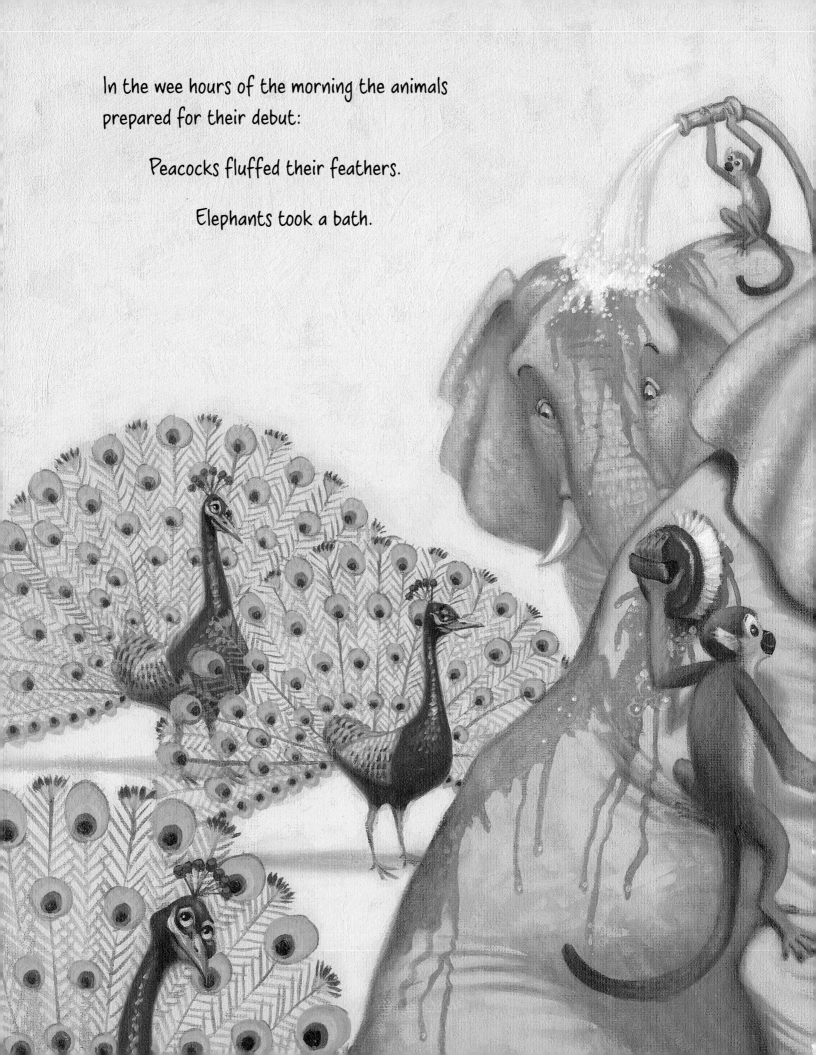

In the wee hours of the morning the animals
prepared for their debut:

Peacocks fluffed their feathers.

Elephants took a bath.

And tuxedo-clad penguins paced.

With butterflies in their stomachs,
the animals took their places.

The gates opened at precisely 10:00 a.m. With baton in hand, Stu conducted the elephants to raise their trunks and play the first note.

Slowly but surely, with cues from Stu, the other animals joined in ...

Squeaks and bellows, gurgles and chirps. . . clucks and pitters, grunts and twitters, croaks, snorts and caws, quacks, squawks, brays and whistles, barks and bleats, coos, hoots, wails and whinnies, squeals, hisses and howls, mews and growls. . .

...all came together in a symphony of sounds!

The music filled the zoo and wafted into the heart of the city.
Everywhere, people stopped and listened.

Reporters and camera crews scurried to capture the phenomenon.

By the time the animals played the final note you could have heard a pin drop.

Until a single clap by a young Maestro followed by another, and another,
became thunderous applause.

That night, the animals were on every news channel, and their concert was replayed over and over to the delight of all, but one.

Tickets to the zoo started selling like hotcakes as people came from all around to hear the animals' symphony.

Day after day, the animals proudly showed off their musical talents for the visitors, and the zoo made national news.

The zoo was getting so much attention that city officials had a change of heart. A press conference was called to announce their decision not to sell it after all.

The animals were thrilled that they had saved their home. In honor of Stu they threw a party!

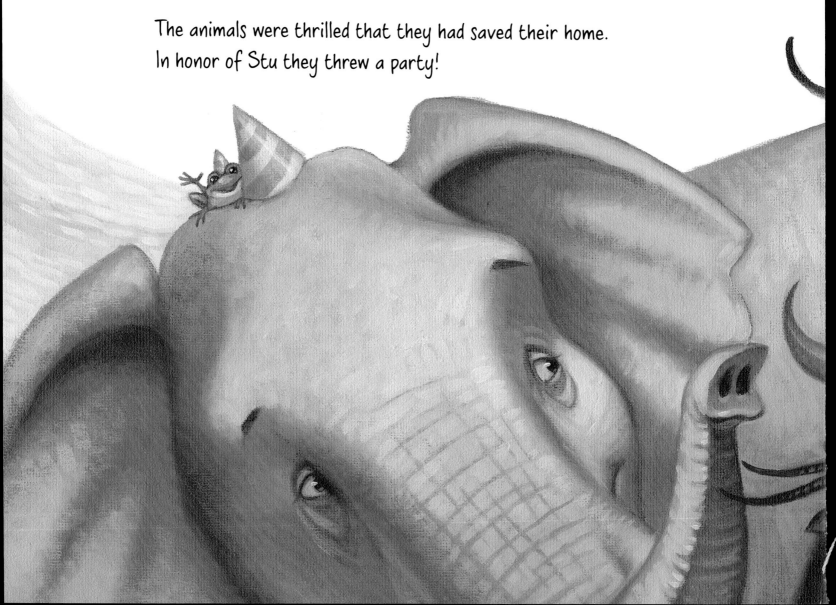

Mr. Cooper was as mad as a wet hen and threw a fit!

But what goes around comes around, and Mr. Cooper now has the job he deserves—he is the official pooper scooper at—where else . . .

...the zoo!

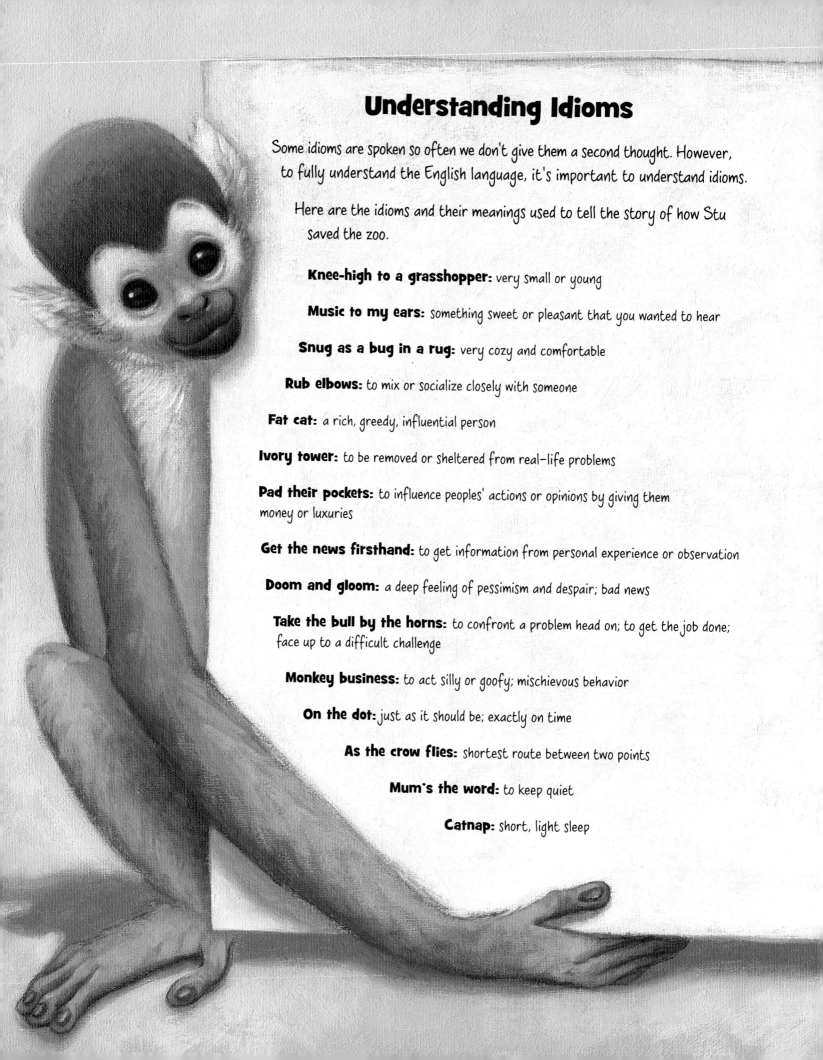

Understanding Idioms

Some idioms are spoken so often we don't give them a second thought. However, to fully understand the English language, it's important to understand idioms.

Here are the idioms and their meanings used to tell the story of how Stu saved the zoo.

Knee-high to a grasshopper: very small or young

Music to my ears: something sweet or pleasant that you wanted to hear

Snug as a bug in a rug: very cozy and comfortable

Rub elbows: to mix or socialize closely with someone

Fat cat: a rich, greedy, influential person

Ivory tower: to be removed or sheltered from real-life problems

Pad their pockets: to influence peoples' actions or opinions by giving them money or luxuries

Get the news firsthand: to get information from personal experience or observation

Doom and gloom: a deep feeling of pessimism and despair; bad news

Take the bull by the horns: to confront a problem head on; to get the job done; face up to a difficult challenge

Monkey business: to act silly or goofy; mischievous behavior

On the dot: just as it should be; exactly on time

As the crow flies: shortest route between two points

Mum's the word: to keep quiet

Catnap: short, light sleep

In an uproar: a lot of commotion and confusion

Coming apart at the seams: to fall apart; about to lose control

Pull yourself together: calm down; get control of your emotions and actions

Making a mountain out of a molehill: to make a major issue out of a minor one; to make something seem much more important than it really is

Have your head in the clouds: to not know what is happening around you because you are not paying attention

Weak at the knees: to have a powerful emotional reaction to something that might make you feel like you will fall over

Get a grip on yourself: to control your emotions

Wear your heart on your sleeve: to allow others to see your feelings or emotions

I'll be a monkey's uncle: to be very surprised; disbelief

Laid eyes on: to see something or someone

Our hands are tied: unable to act because others are in control

All ears: to listen very carefully

Bound and determined: dedicated, devoted; very committed

Dog-tired: exhausted

Wee hours: very late at night or very early in the morning

Butterflies in your stomach: a nervous feeling in your stomach from something stressful or exciting

Slowly but surely: slow, but unstoppable

Able to hear a pin drop: very quiet

Heart of the city: the most central part of the city

Selling like hotcakes: in high demand and selling quickly

Kick up your heels: to celebrate something; to enjoy yourself

Change of heart: a change in attitudes or feelings, usually toward the good

Mad as a wet hen: extremely angry

Threw a fit: to show a lot of anger

What goes around comes around: a person's actions, good or bad, will often have consequences for that person

All's well that ends well: after completing a difficult task or journey, the struggle you went through is forgotten